Tobin Learns to Make Friends

Written and Illustrated
by Diane Murrell

Designed by
Clara Thibeaux

FUTURE HORIZONS INC

All marketing and publishing rights guaranteed to and reserved by

FUTURE HORIZONS INC.

Future Horizons, Inc.
721 W. Abram Street
Arlington, TX 76013

800.489.0727 Toll Free
817.277.0727
817.277.2270 Fax

www.futurehorizons-autism.com
email: info@futurehorizons-autism.com

ISBN 1-885477-79-1

Dedicated to Pat Porcynaluk,
mentor and friend,
for the encouragement and guidance you gave,
as this book came to life.

Tobin

Tobin the red engine was lonely. He had the conductor and the engine driver for friends, but they were so old. It was not the same as another engine friend. But, Tobin was not sure how to make friends.

Shouting

One day Tobin, the little red engine, saw a bright new engine coming down the opposite tracks. He was very excited. A friend for me, he thought.

"Pheep Pheep," he whistled at his loudest as the new engine came by. S C R E E K !
Tobin's whistle was so loud that the other train jumped. The coal in the coal cars spilled onto the tracks when the engine jumped. The guard put his hands over his ears because the whistle hurt his head.

"Quickly, quickly, clickety, clickety," rushed the cars behind the startled engine. "Let's get away from that loud noise!" The engine raced by quickly and did not see Tobin's sad face.

"Oh dear," said Tobin's conductor. "Tobin, you cannot shout at someone beside you. It alarms them and they move away because the sound is too loud."

Crowding

"I will try again to make a friend," Tobin said. That morning, the station-master asked Tobin's driver to push old cars down the track to the engine shed to be painted.

Soon, Limon came to help. Tobin was so thrilled to have a friend, that he jumped off his tracks sideways.

Tobin landed right bang splat on top of Limon's rails. Limon had no time to stop and his nose hit Tobin's nose. "Ouch!" shouted Limon. "My nose is squashed metal! You're in my space and I can't work with you so close to me."
"Oh, Tobin," said his driver. "If you want a friend, you must not get right up in his face."

Tobin really did want to have friends.

Sharing

One day, all the engines in the station had no work to do. It was like recess. "Let's play Follow the Leader," shouted Jason, a big yellow train. They all followed him round and round, fast and slow. "Let's play Pokemon® cards," said Tobin.

"No," cried the engines. "We still want to play Follow the Leader."

Tobin kept on arguing, "I want to play Pokemon® cards." The other engines were enjoying their game too much to listen to him.

Tobin's driver came out of the roundhouse. "Tobin," he said, "to be a friend, sometimes you have to play what the others want to play and think about them first."

Borrowing

Each morning, Tobin woke up early in the roundhouse, where the engines slept. One morning, he could not find his whistle. He chugged quietly over to Sara, the pink engine, who was still asleep. He took her whistle without asking.

When Sara woke up, she was scared to not have a whistle. Then, after she heard Tobin blowing her whistle, she became angry.

"You did not ask me if you could borrow my whistle," Sara said. "Now I am mad. I don't want to be your friend."

Interrupting

The stationmaster and Tobin's driver were discussing a new route they had been given. Tobin tried to interrupt them. "Excuse me," he said, jumping up and down.

"Just a minute, Tobin," said his driver, waving his hand at Tobin.

"Excuse me. Excuse me. Excuse me. Ex..."

Tobin's driver and stationmaster could not hear their conversation because Tobin was so loud and would not stop repeating the words "excuse me".

The driver became angry. "Tobin, you're not being polite," he said. "After you say 'excuse me' one time, you should stop talking and wait silently."

Taking Turns

A week after Tobin returned Sara's whistle and said "I'm sorry",
she decided to play with him again.
They each tried to see who could blow the biggest puff of smoke.

Tobin became so excited about puffing out clouds of smoke that he forgot all about Sara. He took all the turns and wouldn't give Sara a turn. Sara chugged away down the tracks to play with someone else. She wanted to play with someone who remembered to give her a turn, too.

Being Kind

A new little engine came by. "Oh look," said Tobin. "You are so tiny." The little engine was upset that Tobin said he was so tiny. It hurt his feelings.

"Say something nice," the engine driver said. "How about saying, Tiny, I bet you can fit through any tunnel and never get stuck." So Tobin did, and Tiny felt better.

Good Manners

The Zoo train was coming. "Remember, no jumping. You'll frighten the animals," said the engine driver.

Tobin did not jump and he remembered what Sara said about taking turns. He waited in line to see the animals.

The Zoo engine needed to go to the breakdown shed for some work.

"Tobin, you have shown such good manners today. You were quiet around the animals and did not jump. I like how you waited for your turn, too. Would you like to pull the zoo train to its next stop while the engine is in the shed?"
Tobin was proud. The engines in the yard were happy to see Tobin get a reward for his good behavior.

Rules

One day, as Tobin chugged along the line, he saw a red light flashing. It was the signal to stop. Tobin was having such a good time going fast, he did not want to stop.

He did not obey the red light and ran on. Suddenly, Tobin started falling through the air. The bridge track over a small valley was broken.

Tobin landed on his nose. The sheep came up to stare at him.
His engine driver was upset that Tobin disobeyed the red light.

He walked a long way to a telephone to call for help to pull
Tobin out.

A crane came and pulled him out and set him back on the tracks.

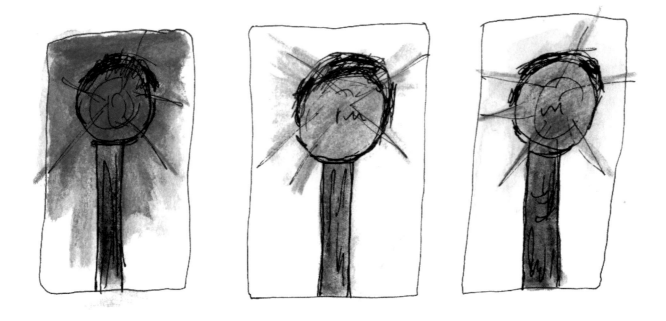

Tobin learned another lesson. Rules are there to protect us.

"Tobin", said the engine driver. "Rules keep you out of trouble. They also help you make friends and help you keep friends."

If you want to make friends, or keep friends, remember:

Don't shout too loud and frighten friends

Don't crowd friends and get too close to their face

Share in your friends' games

Don't borrow things without asking first

Take turns

Don't interrupt

Use kind words

Have good manners

Obey rules

Tobin does not always get it right. Sometimes he gets so excited, he forgets a rule. But because he tries very hard, all the other engines are his friends now.

Diane Murrell was born in Northern Ireland and grew up in a small town named Ballymena, where her family still lives today. She now resides and works in Houston, Texas, with her four intrepid boys, who attend four different magnet schools. One of her sons has Aspergers, and was the inspiration for this book.

With two kilns at her house, Diane throws pots and leads clay workshops for atypical and neurotypical kids. She grows roses to avoid housework and dances Swing and Western to avoid pulling her hair out.

Diane is currently working on her next children's book.

Photo by John Hozack